Let's Enjoy Masterpieces!

GRADE 2

A Dog of Flanders

龍龍與忠狗

Original Author　Ouida
Adaptors　　　　David Desmond O'Flaherty
Illustrator　　　Petra Hanzak

WORDS
450

MP3

Let's Enjoy Masterpieces!

All the beautiful fairy tales and masterpieces that you have encountered during your childhood remain as warm memories in your adulthood. This time, let's indulge in the world of masterpieces through English. You can enjoy the depth and beauty of original works, which you can't enjoy through Chinese translations.

The stories are easy for you to understand because of your familiarity with them. When you enjoy reading, your ability to understand English will also rapidly improve.

This series of Let's Enjoy Masterpieces is a special reading comprehension booster program, devised to improve reading comprehension for beginners whose command of English is not satisfactory, or who are elementary, middle, and high school students. With this program, you can enjoy reading masterpieces in English with fun and efficiency.

This carefully planned program is composed of 5 levels, from the beginner level of 350 words to the intermediate and advanced levels of 1,000 words. With this program's level-by-level system, you are able to read famous texts in English and to savor the true pleasure of the world's language.

The program is well conceived, composed of reader-friendly explanations of English expressions and grammar, quizzes to help the student learn vocabulary and understand the meaning of the texts, and fabulous illustrations that adorn every page. In addition, with our "Guide to Listening," not only is reading comprehension enhanced but also listening comprehension skills are highlighted.

In the audio recording of the book, texts are vividly read by professional American actors. The texts are rewritten, according to the levels of the readers by an expert editorial staff of native speakers, on the basis of standard American English with the ministry of education recommended vocabulary. Therefore, it will be of great help even for all the students that want to learn English.

Please indulge yourself in the fun of reading and listening to English through Let's Enjoy Masterpieces.

薇達

Ouida
(1839-1908)

Ouida was an English woman novelist born in England to an English father and a French mother. Her real name was Marie Louise de la Ramee, and she derived her pen name from her own baby-talk nickname for "Louise." She started to write novels when she was in her twenties. She moved to Italy when she was 30 and never returned to London.

Ouida wrote a lot of novels about animals, because she was an animal lover and she also kept several dogs in her house. She became famous and wealthy when she began to write novels about children.

Although she was successful, she did not manage her money well and died in poverty. Ouida remained single for life and wrote a large number of great works like *The Nurnberg Stove* and *A Dog of Flanders*.

A Dog of Flanders

The main character, Nello, lived happily with his grandfather and adopted dog Patrasche even though he was poor.

Nello was talented and wanted to be an artist. He did his best to finish his painting for the village art competition, but his luck turned when his grandfather died and his work was not accepted. His life then became desperate.

He had a strong desire to see Rubens's work in the cathedral, so one Christmas Eve he and Patrasche went to the cathedral. He finally saw one of his favorite paintings by Rubens. However, the next morning people found a dead boy with his dog in front of the painting.

This story is about poor people and compassion for animals. Even today, it still has a great number of readers because of the natural features of Belgium, the delicate descriptions of the characters, and the well-structured plot.

This story is set in Antwerp, which is the second largest city in Belgium. There are lots of interesting places for sightseeing and for enjoying nature in Antwerp, for example, an antique train station in Marx Square and a small beautiful village named Hoboken.

However, the most famous place is the Notre Dame Cathedral, which is the main setting of this story. There are some original Rubens's paintings in the cathedral, including "Elevation of the Cross" and "Descent From the Cross" that Nello had a strong desire to see.

HOW TO USE THIS BOOK
本書使用說明

① Original English texts

It is easy to understand the meaning of the text, because the text is divided phrase by phrase and sentence by sentence.

② Explanation of the vocabulary

The words and expressions that include vocabulary above the elementary level are clearly defined.

③ Response notes

Spaces are included in the book so you can take notes about what you don't understand or what you want to remember.

④ One point lesson

In-depth analyses of major grammar points and expressions help you to understand sentences with difficult grammar.

∩ *Audio Recording*

In the audio recording, native speakers narrate the texts in standard American English. By combining the written words and the audio recording, you can listen to English with great ease.

Audio books have been popular in Britain and America for many decades. They allow the listener to experience the proper word pronunciation and sentence intonation that add important meaning and drama to spoken English. Students will benefit from listening to the recording twenty or more times.

After you are familiar with the text and recording, listen once more with your eyes closed to check your listening comprehension. Finally, after you can listen with your eyes closed and understand every word and every sentence, you are then ready to mimic the native speaker.

Then you should make a recording by reading the text yourself. Then play both recordings to compare your oral skills with those of a native speaker.

HOW TO IMPROVE
READING ABILITY
如何增進英文閱讀能力

① *Catch key words*

Read the key words in the sentences and practice catching the gist of the meaning of the sentence. You might question how working with a few important words could enhance your reading ability. However, it's quite effective. If you continue to use this method, you will find out that the key words and your knowledge of people and situations enables you to understand the sentence.

② *Divide long sentences*

Read in chunks of meaning, dividing sentences into meaningful chunks of information. In the book, chunks are arranged in sentences according to meaning. If you consider the sentences backwards or grammatically, your reading speed will be slow and you will find it difficult to listen to English.

You are ready to move to a more sophisticated level of comprehension when you find that narrowly focusing on chunks is irritating. Instead of considering the chunks, you will make it a habit to read the sentence from the beginning to the end to figure out the meaning of the whole.

3 Make inferences and assumptions

Making inferences and assumptions is part of your ability. If you don't know, try to guess the meaning of the words. Although you don't know all the words in context, don't go straight to the dictionary. Developing an ability to make inferences in the context is important.

The first way to figure out the meaning of a word is from its context. If you cannot make head or tail out of the meaning of a word, look at what comes before or after it. Ask yourself what can happen in such a situation. Make your best guess as to the word's meaning. Then check the explanations of the word in the book or look up the word in a dictionary.

4 Read a lot and reread the same book many times

There is no shortcut to mastering English. Only if you do a lot of reading will you make your way to the summit. Read fun and easy books with an average of less than one new word per page. Try to immerse yourself in English as often as you can.

Spend time "swimming" in English. Language learning research has shown that immersing yourself in English will help you improve your English, even though you may not be aware of what you're learning.

CONTENTS

A Dog of Flanders

龍龍與忠狗

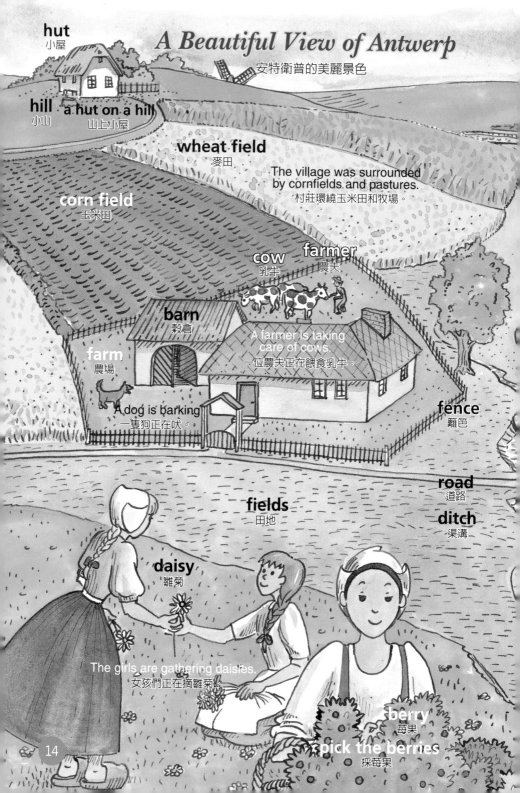

A Beautiful View of Antwerp
安特衛普的美麗景色

hut
小屋

hill
小山

a hut on a hill
山上小屋

wheat field
麥田

The village was surrounded by cornfields and pastures.
村莊環繞玉米田和牧場。

corn field
玉米田

cow
乳牛

farmer
農夫

barn
穀倉

farm
農場

A farmer is taking care of cows.
一位農夫正在餵食乳牛。

A dog is barking.
一隻狗正在吠。

fence
籬笆

road
道路

fields
田地

ditch
渠溝

daisy
雛菊

The girls are gathering daisies.
女孩們正在摘雛菊。

berry
莓果

pick the berries
採莓果

14

Before You Read

windmill
風車

forest
森林

city hall
市政廳

CITY HALL

pasture
牧場

clock
鐘

villager
村民

townspeople
兩民

roof
屋頂

At the top of the church, there was an old clock.
教堂屋頂有一座老舊的鐘。

window
窗戶

shops
商店

Cafe

grandfather
祖父

grandson
孫子

collect money
收錢

cart
小貨車

sell the farmers' milk
販賣農夫的牛奶
pull the cart 拉小貨車

harness
挽具

15

· Chapter One ·

Nello and Patrasche

Although[1] Nello was a boy and Patrasche was a dog, they had a special[2] friendship[3], closer to[4] brotherhood[5].

They were both the same age[6]. Yet[7], one seemed[8] old and the other was young. They spent[9] all of their time together. Their home was a little hut[10] on the edge of[11] a small village[12].

1. **although** [ɒl`ðou] (conj.) 雖然;儘管
2. **special** [`speʃəl] (a.) 特別的
3. **friendship** [`frendʃɪp] (n.) 友誼;友情
4. **closer to** 接近
5. **brotherhood** [`brʌðərhud] (n.) 兄弟關係;手足之情
6. **age** [eɪdʒ] (n.) 年齡
7. **yet** [jet] (adv.) 然而
8. **seem** [siːm] (v.) 看來好像;似乎
9. **spend** [spend] (v.) 花費（時間、精力）(spend-spent-spent)
10. **hut** [hʌt] (n.) 小屋
11. **on the edge of** 在……旁邊
12. **village** [`vɪlɪdʒ] (n.) 村莊

The village was near¹³ Antwerp. It was surrounded by¹⁴ cornfields¹⁵ and pastures¹⁶.

In the center of¹⁷ the village was a big windmill¹⁸. A gray church stood across from¹⁹ the windmill.

At the top of the church, there was an old clock. The clock rang²⁰ every hour on the hour²¹. It made²² a strange, empty²³ sound. To the villagers, it seemed like²⁴ the saddest sound in the world.

13. **near** [nɪr] (prep.) 在……附近
14. **be surrounded by . . .** 四周環繞……
15. **cornfield** [ˈkɔːrnˌfiːld] (n.) 玉米田
16. **pasture** [ˈpæstʃər] (n.) 牧場
17. **in the center of** 在……的中心
18. **windmill** [ˈwɪndˌmɪl] (n.) 風車
19. **across from** 在……的對面
20. **ring** [rɪŋ] (v.) 鳴；響
21. **every hour on the hour** 每小時的整點
22. **make a sound** 發出聲音
23. **empty** [ˈɛmptɪ] (a.) 空洞的；無意義的
24. **seem like** 似乎像是

Nello and Patrasche lived with a very old man. This man, Jehan Daas, was Nello's grandfather.

He had once[1] been a soldier[2]. Sadly[3], he was wounded[4] in a war and was now crippled[5]. When Jehan Daas was eighty years old, his only[6] daughter died.

1. **once** [wʌns] (adv.)
   曾經；一次
2. **soldier** [`souldʒər] (n.) 軍人
3. **sadly** [`sædli] (adv.)
   不幸地；令人傷心地
4. **wound** [wuːnd] (v.)
   使受傷；傷害
5. **cripple** [`krɪpəl] (v.)
   使成跛子；使殘廢

6. **only** [`ounli] (a.)
   唯一的；僅有的
7. **have no choice but**
   只有此選擇
8. **take care of** 照顧……
9. **each other** 彼此
10. **enough** [ɪ`nʌf] (a.)
    足夠的；充足的
11. **as for** 至於；說到

The old man had no choice but[7] to take care of[8] his daughter's son.

The old man and the little boy lived happily together. They were very poor, but they had each other[9]. That was enough[10].

As for[11] Patrasche, he made the old man and little Nello happier.

◆ He **had** once **been** a soldier. 他以前當過軍人。

had + 過去分詞：過去完成式，表示在過去某個特定時間之前，一個已經完成的行為動作。

e.g. I **had met** her somewhere before.
我以前在某處曾看過她。

Patrasche, a dog of Flanders, was a slave[1] once. His owner[2] forced[3] him to pull[4] a cart full of[5] iron[6].

One summer day, Patrasche was very thirsty when he was working. But he wasn't allowed[7] to stop and drink.

1. **slave** [sleɪv] (n.) 奴隸
2. **owner** [ˋoʊnər] (n.) 主人；所有人
3. **force A to** 強迫 A……
4. **pull** [pʊl] (v.) 拉；拖曳
5. **full of** 充滿……
6. **iron** [ˋaɪərn] (n.) 鐵
7. **allow** [əˋlaʊ] (v.) 准許；允許
8. **dizzy** [ˋdɪzi] (a.) 頭暈的
9. **fall down** 倒下 (fall-fell-fallen)
10. **beat** [biːt] (v.) 打；敲打 (beat-beat-beat)
11. **kick** [kɪk] (v.) 踢
12. **ditch** [dɪtʃ] (n.) 溝渠
13. **let + A + 原型動詞** 讓 A ……
14. **such** [sʌtʃ] (a.) 這樣的
15. **drag** [dræg] (v.) 拉；拖 (drag-dragged-dragged)

After some walking, he became dizzy[8] and fell down[9]. His owner ran up to him and beat[10] him. Patrasche couldn't move. His owner kicked[11] him into a ditch[12] and went away.

After some time, an old man and a little boy saw Patrasche.

"We can't let[13] such[14] a beautiful dog die," said the old man. He dragged[15] the big dog back to his hut.

This was how old Jehan Daas, little Nello and Patrasche first met.

One Point Lesson

This was how old Jehan Daas, little Nello and Patrasche first met.
這就是老耶漢・達斯、小龍龍和阿忠相識的情景。

This is how . . . ：在此句型中，how 引介一個描述事實的子句。

e.g. **This is how** she always treats me.
這是她對待我的方式。

The old man and little Nello took great care of Patrasche. More than[1] this, they loved him. They patted[2] him softly[3] on the head. They made a bed for him to sleep in.

This was the first time for Patrasche to feel love. It seemed strange to him yet wonderful. He was determined to[4] get well[5] soon and repay[6] them for their kindness[7]. He wanted to take care of them.

1. **more than** 多於……
2. **pat** [pæt] (v.) 輕拍；拍撫
3. **softly** [ˋsɒːftli] (adv.) 輕輕地；溫柔地
4. **be determined to** 決心要……
5. **get well** 康復
6. **repay** [rɪˋpeɪ] (v.) 償還；報答
7. **kindness** [ˋkaɪndnɪs] (n.) 仁慈
8. **finally** [ˋfaɪnəli] (adv.) 最後；終於
9. **bark** [bɑːrk] (v.) 吠叫
10. **stretch** [stretʃ] (v.) 伸直；伸長
11. **joy** [dʒɔɪ] (n.) 高興；歡欣
12. **hug** [hʌg] (v.) 擁抱；緊抱 (hug-hugged-hugged)

When he finally[8] stood up, he barked[9] and stretched[10] his legs. Nello and the old man danced for joy[11] and hugged[12] the dog.

◊ They patted him softly **on the head.**
他們輕柔地拍他的頭。

on the + 受詞：表示觸摸或拍打的動詞（hit, pat, touch），後面需接介係詞 on。on 可以表示物體擱置在某個水平的表面上，或是附著在某個垂直的表面上。

e.g. He hit me **on the head**. 他打我的頭。

Patrasche walked over to[1] the cart. He knew that the old man used that cart to make money[2].

Old Jehan Daas carried[3] farmers' milk cans to the market[4] in Antwerp. He sold[5] the milk for the farmers and brought the empty cans back[6]. The farmers then gave him some of their profits[7].

Patrasche decided[8] that the old man would never again pull such a heavy cart. Patrasche stood by[9] that cart for days. Finally, he started to pull the cart with his teeth.

1. **walk over to** 走到……
2. **make money** 賺錢
3. **carry** [`kæri] (v.) 運送；運載 (carry-carried-carried)
4. **market** [`mɑːrkɪt] (n.) 市場
5. **sell** [sel] (v.) 販賣 (sell-sold-sold)
6. **bring A back** 帶 A 回來 (bring-brought-brought)
7. **profit** [`prɑːfɪt] (n.) 利益；紅利

"Alright, alright!" called old Jehan Daas.

"I see that I can't persuade[10] you not to pull the cart."

The old man put a harness[11] around Patrasche's shoulders. Patrasche was glad to[12] do the work. This was easy work compared to[13] what he used to[14] do.

8. **decide** [dɪˋsaɪd] (v.) 決定
9. **stand by** 站在……旁
10. **persuade** [pərˋsweɪd] (v.) 說服;勸服
11. **harness** [ˋhɑːrnɪs] (n.) 挽具
12. **be glad to** 很高興去……
13. **compared to** 與……比較
14. **used to** 過去曾;過去常

A Choose the words that are not in this picture.

hut   crippled   friendship   cart   dizzy

B Fill in the blanks with antonyms.

1 Patrasche had ever felt _____.

⇔hatred

2 Patrasche decided to _____ the cart for old Jehan Daas.   ⇔push

3 Old Jehan Daas sold the milk and brought the _____ cans back.

⇔ full

C True or False.

T F ❶ Jehan Daas was Nello's father.

T F ❷ Jehan Daas wanted Patrasche to work for him.

T F ❸ Jehan Daas carried farmers' milk cans to the market in Antwerp.

T F ❹ Jehan Daas had once been a farmer.

T F ❺ Nello and Jehan Dass were poor, but they were happy.

D Fill in the blanks with the given words.

church   surrounded   clock   windmill

It was near Antwerp and was ❶ _____ by cornfields and pastures. In the center of the village was a big ❷ _____. A little gray ❸ _____ stood across from the ❷ _____. At the top of the ❸ _____, there was an old ❹ _____.

Chapter Two

A Few Years Later

Old Jehan Daas became very weak. It was impossible[1] for him to go out with the cart anymore[2]. So little Nello collected[3] money at the markets.

1. **impossible** [ɪmˈpɑːsəbəl] (a.) 不可能的
2. **anymore** [ˌeniˈmɔːr] (adv.) 不再；再也不
3. **collect** [kəˈlekt] (v.) 收集；收款
4. **honestly** [ˈɑːnɪstli] (adv.) 誠實地
5. **be happy to** 很高興……
6. **do business with** 和……做生意 （business：生意）
7. **fine** [faɪn] (a.) 好的；優秀的
8. **hardworking** [ˌhɑːrdˈwɜːrkɪŋ] (a.) 努力工作的
9. **shake off** 擺脫
10. **with delight** 欣喜地 （delight：欣喜）

He worked hard and honestly[4]. The farmers were happy to[5] do business with[6] such a fine[7], hardworking[8] boy.

In the afternoon, the two came back home. Patrasche would shake off[9] his harness and bark with delight[10].

Nello would talk to his grandfather about the day's business. They would all eat their simple[11] meals[12] together. Old Jehan Daas would tell funny[13] stories about the days when he was a soldier. They would all laugh and have fun[14].

11. **simple** [ˋsɪmpəl] (a.) 簡單的
12. **meal** [miːl] (n.) 餐

13. **funny** [ˋfʌni] (a.) 有趣的；滑稽的
14. **have fun** 過得開心

One Point Lesson

◆ Patrasche **would** shake off his harness and bark with delight.
阿忠會掙開挽帶，欣喜地吠叫。

---

would：用來描述過去的習慣，此時其意義和 used to 一樣。

e.g. Sometimes he **would** ask me about my father.
有時他會問我我爸爸的事。

🎧 7

Many years passed[1] and they were still[2] happy. Flanders is not a beautiful place. There is not much to see besides[3] cornfields and farms.

However, its simple beauty is enough to be enjoyed by a boy and his dog. These two couldn't imagine[4] a more beautiful place in the world.

1. **pass** [pæs] (v.) 度過
2. **still** [stɪl] (adv.) 仍然；還是
3. **besides** [bɪˋsaɪdz] (prep.) 除……之外
4. **imagine** [ɪˋmædʒɪn] (v.) 想像
5. **hard** [hɑːrd] (a.) 艱難的；刻苦的

It's true that life was harder[5] in the wintertime[6]. But they never complained[7] about being cold.

Their simple hut was warm enough. They didn't mind[8] that they were poor. They had each other and that was enough.

6. **wintertime** [ˋwɪntərˌtaɪm] (n.) 冬季

7. **complain** [kəmˋpleɪn] (v.) 抱怨；發牢騷

8. **mind** [maɪnd] (v.) 介意；留意

There was only one thing that Patrasche didn't like.

Antwerp is a city full of old churches. Everywhere[1] you looked in Antwerp, you could see a church. Inside the churches, you could find the masterpieces[2] of Rubens.

Rubens was a great artist, a great master[3]. He was the only person whom the local[4] people worshipped[5].

1. **everywhere** [`evriwer] (adv.) 到處；無論何處
2. **masterpiece** [`mæstərpi:s] (n.) 傑作；名作
3. **master** [`mæstər] (n.) 名家；能手
4. **local** [`loukəl] (a.) 當地的；本地的
5. **worship** [`wɜːrʃɪp] (v.) 崇拜；敬仰
6. **trouble** [`trʌbəl] (n.) 煩惱；焦慮
7. **ad well** 也；同樣地
8. **disappear** [ˌdɪsə`pɪr] (v.) 消失；不見

Now, the trouble[6] with Patrasche was this: Nello worshipped Rubens as well[7]. The little boy would often disappear[8] into the churches. The poor dog had to wait outside in the cold.

When the little boy came back, he always seemed very sad. "If only I could see them, Patrasche!" he would say. What were "they"? Patrasche had no idea.

One Point Lesson

He was the only person **whom** the local people worshipped.
他是當地人唯一崇拜的人。

名詞 + **whom**：whom 引介限定關係子句。

e.g. That is the boy **whom** I saw on the bus this morning.
那是我今天早上在公車上看到的男孩。

They were two large covered[1] paintings[2] at a church.

The little boy was crying.

"It is so terrible[3] that I can't see those paintings. Just because I'm poor and I can't pay[4]! Rubens painted those for everyone to see. Not just for the rich[5]."

---

1. **covered** [ˋkʌvərd] (a.)
   遮蔽著的；用布蓋著的
2. **painting** [ˋpeɪntɪŋ] (n.) 繪畫
3. **terrible** [ˋterəbəl] (a.)
   令人討厭的；極差的
4. **pay** [peɪ] (v.) 付款；支付
5. **the rich** 富人
6. **silver coin** 銀幣
7. **in order to** 為了……

8. **save** [seɪv] (v.)
   節省；儲存
9. **passionately**
   [ˋpæʃənətli] (adv.)
   熱情地；熱烈地
10. **through** [θruː] (prep.)
    通過；經過
11. **be amazed by**
    對……很吃驚
12. **notice** [ˋnoutɪs] (v.) 注意到

He couldn't see them and Patrasche couldn't help him. People had to pay a silver coin[6] in order to[7] see them. That was more money than Nello could save[8] in a month.

Little Nello loved art passionately[9]. When the little boy walked through[10] the town, he was amazed by[11] the beauty he saw. He would look at a simple church or a windmill and notice[12] its beauty.

One Point Lesson

◆ That was **more** money **than** Nello could save in a month.
那比龍龍一個月能夠存的錢還要多。

---

more . . . than：指數量更多的人或物，也可以形成形容詞或副詞的比較級。

e.g. The next war will be **more** terrible **than** could be imagined.
下一場戰爭將會比想像中的更可怕。

Although Nello had never gone to school, he was nonetheless[1] a very smart child. No one[2] had taught him how to[3] read. No one had taught him how to draw[4]. In fact[5], no one had taught him anything. He had what people call[6] "genius[7]."

No one knew it. He didn't even know it himself. Only Patrasche had an idea[8]. That big, smart old dog noticed the boy drawing on stones. He often watched Nello's face brighten[9] when he saw a wonderful sunset[10].

1. **nonetheless** [ˌnʌnðəˈles] (adv.) 但是；仍然
2. **no one** 沒有人
3. **how to** 如何……
4. **draw** [drɔː] (v.) 繪畫；畫圖 (draw-drew-drawn)
5. **in fact** 事實上
6. **what people call** 人們所謂……
7. **genius** [ˈdʒiːniəs] (n.) 天資；天賦
8. **have an idea** 知道；了解
9. **brighten** [ˈbraɪtn] (v.) 露出喜色；變明亮
10. **sunset** [ˈsʌnset] (n.) 夕陽；日落

One Point Lesson

◊ That big, smart old dog **noticed the boy drawing on stones.**

那隻聰明的大狗注意到男孩在石頭上畫畫。

---

notice + 詞 + V-ing：注意到……，後面加上 V-ing 表示強調當時動作的正在進行。

e.g. The teacher **noticed Jenny** not **listening** to him.

老師注意到珍妮沒有在聽他說話。

The boy secretly[1] wished[2] to become a great artist. He never told any person this, however. And Jehan Daas had other ideas for him.

He wanted his little grandson[3] to become a farmer. He felt that all men should become simple farmers. To the old man, becoming a farmer was the greatest success[4] in the world.

However, Nello didn't want to become a farmer at all[5]. He couldn't tell the old man that. It would break his heart[6].

Sometimes in the evenings, Nello would whisper[7] about his dreams[8] into Patrasche's ears. Patrasche was the only one that would understand[9] him. No one else would. So he and Patrasche kept it a secret[10].

1. **secretly** [ˋsiːkrɪtli] (adv.) 秘密地；偷偷地
2. **wish** [wɪʃ] (v.) 希望；想要
3. **grandson** [ˋɡrændˏsʌn] (n.) 孫子
4. **success** [səkˋses] (n.) 成功
5. **not . . . at all** 一點也不⋯⋯
6. **break one's heart** 傷⋯⋯的心
7. **whisper** [ˋwɪspər] (v.) 低語；耳語
8. **dream** [driːm] (n.) 夢想；理想
9. **understand** [ˏʌndərˋstænd] (v.) 理解；了解 (understand-understood-understood)
10. **keep it a secret** 保守秘密 (keep-kept-kept)

A Recombine the letters to fill in the blanks.

1 Nello was such an (n, h, e, t, o, s) boy. ⇨ _____

2 Nello would often (p, p, a, d, s, r, i, a, e) into the churches. ⇨ _____

3 Nello and Patrasche couldn't (a, i, g, e, m, n, i) a more beautiful place than Flanders. ⇨ _____

4 Life was harder in the wintertime, but their simple hut was warm (g, e, o, n, h, u). ⇨ _____

B True or False.

T F **1** Only Patrasche knew about Nello's dreams.

T F **2** Nello and Patrasche hated the fact that they were poor.

T F **3** Nello did a good job at school.

C Fill in names according to the descriptions.

❶ He became very weak. It was impossible for him to pull the cart anymore.

_____

❷ When he came out of the church, he always looked very sad.

_____

❸ He was the only person whom people in Antwerp worshipped.

_____

D Choose the correct answer.

❶ Nello couldn't see the Rubens paintings because

_____

(a) his eyes were very weak.

(b) the church doors were always closed.

(c) he couldn't pay to see them.

❷ Jehan Daas wanted Nello to be a farmer because

_____

(a) he felt a farmer was a successful job.

(b) Nello was good at farming.

(c) a farmer could earn more money than a soldier.

Before You Read

cloud
雲

sunset
夕陽

The sun is setting.
太陽要下山了。

leather wallet
皮夾

the miller
磨坊主

quite a rich man
相當富有的人

Alois is putting her arms around Patrashe.
阿露薏絲抱著阿忠。

footprint
腳印

portrait
畫像

chalk
粉筆

paper
紙

Nello is drawing a portrait of Alois.
龍龍正在畫阿露薏絲的畫像。

in black and white
白紙黑筆

He wanted to be a great artist.
他要成為一位偉大的畫家。

charcoal
炭筆

puppet
玩偶

gift
禮物

easel
畫架

watercolors
水彩顏料

paintbrush
畫筆

palette
調色盤

42

whisper
私語
A girl is whispering in her friend's ear.
一位女孩正在她的好友耳旁私語。

call out
大叫
A boy is calling out.
一位男孩正在大叫。

announce
宣佈
The winner will be announced on Christmas Eve.
獲勝者將於耶誕前夕宣佈。

slip
滑跤
A boy is slipping on the icy road.
一位男孩在結冰的路上跌跤了。

climb
爬
A boy is climbing up a tree.
一位男孩正在爬樹。

scratch
抓；劃
A dog is scratching at the ground. 一隻狗正在抓地。

set fire
生火
A man is setting fire to a stove.
一位男人在爐灶生火。

put out the fire
滅火
People are putting out the fire.
人們正在滅火。

follow
跟隨
A dog is following a girl.
一隻狗跟著一位女孩。

pay one's respect
表達敬意
A woman is paying her respect at a funeral.
一位女人在葬禮上致意。

rest
休息
A man is resting on a fallen tree.
一位男人在倒下的樹上休息。

answer the door
應門
A girl is answering the door. 一位女孩去應門。

· Chapter Three ·

A Little Girl 🎧12

Eventually[1], Nello told his secret to another[2] person. That person was a little girl who lived nearby[3]. Her name was Alois. She lived in a red mill[4].

Her father, Baas Cogez, was the miller[5]. He was quite[6] a rich man. Little Alois was a pretty girl. She had dark eyes, and bright, rosy[7] cheeks[8].

1. **eventually** [ɪˋventʃuəli] (adv.) 最後；終於
2. **another** [əˋnʌðər] (a.) 另一個的；另外的
3. **nearby** [ˋnɪrˌbaɪ] (adv.) 在附近
4. **mill** [mɪl] (n.) 磨坊
5. **miller** [ˋmɪlər] (n.) 磨坊主人
6. **quite** [kwaɪt] (adv.) 完全；相當
7. **rosy** [ˋrouzi] (a.) 玫瑰色的；紅潤的
8. **cheek** [tʃiːk] (n.) 臉頰
9. **gather** [ˋgæðər] (v.) 摘；採集
10. **daisy** [ˋdeɪzi] (n.) 雛菊
11. **berry** [ˋberi] (n.) 莓果
12. **marry** [ˋmæri] (v.) 娶；和……結婚

Little Alois often played with Nello and Patrasche. They gathered[9] daisies[10] and berries[11] in the field. They went up to the old gray church together. They ran in the snow.

Alois was the richest little girl in the village. People in the town dreamed that their sons would marry[12] her.

When Nello, Alois and Patrasche were in the fields, Nello drew a portrait[1] of Alois.

At that moment[2] Baas Cogez was walking through the field. When he saw Nello and Alois there, he became very angry.

"Alois," he called out[3].

"Why are you playing here? Go home quickly[4]!"

1. **portrait** [`pɔːrtrɪt] (n.) 肖像；畫像
2. **at that moment** 在那一刻
3. **call out** 大喊
4. **quickly** [`kwɪkli] (adv.) 即刻；馬上
5. **pick up** 拾起
6. **drawing** [`drɒːɪŋ] (n.) 圖畫；描繪
7. **turn** 形容詞 變成……
8. **foolish** [`fuːlɪʃ] (a.) 愚蠢的；傻的
9. **as** [əz] (prep.) 作為；當作
10. **gift** [gɪft] (n.) 禮物
11. **walk away** 離開
12. **across** [ə`krɒːs] (prep.) 橫越；穿過

Baas Cogez then picked up[5] the drawing[6] of Alois. Nello's face turned[7] red.

"I draw everything I see," he said.

"Here. I'll give you this silver coin for your drawing. I think spending your time drawing things is foolish[8]. But I do like this picture a lot."

"Please take this drawing as[9] a gift[10]," Nello said.

Nello walked away[11] across[12] the fields.

"I could have seen the Rubens paintings with that money," he said to Patrasche. "But I just couldn't sell her picture."

🎧14

Baas Cogez returned[1] to his mill that night.

"Nello shouldn't play with Alois so much," he said to his wife.

"He's fifteen years old now and she's twelve. In a few years[2], he'll probably[3] want to marry her. He's just a poor boy who's never been to school."

"But he's a good and honest boy," said his wife.

1. **return** [rɪˋtɜːrn] (v.) 返回；回歸
2. **in a few years** 幾年之後
3. **probably** [ˋprɑːbəbli] (adv.) 大概；或許
4. **agree** [əˋgriː] (v.) 同意；贊同
5. **landowner** [ˋlændˏounər] (n.) 地主
6. **keep A away** 使 A 離開
7. **if not** 若非如此
8. **send** [send] (v.) 使進入；派遣；打發 (send-sent-sent)
9. **far away** 遙遠地
10. **convent** [ˋkɑːnvent] (n.) 女修道院

"I agree[4]," said the miller. "But he spends all of his time drawing. He'll never be a landowner[5] like me. Listen to me. You keep that boy away[6] from Alois. If not[7], then I'll send[8] her far away[9] to a convent[10]."

The next day, she told Alois not to play with Nello anymore. Alois, however, didn't listen to her.

A few days later, Alois went to see Nello as usual[1]. When she put her hand in his, Nello said,

"No, Alois. We shouldn't make your father angry. He doesn't want you to play with poor boys. He is a good man. We should obey[2] him."

Nello was very sad to say this. The world was an uglier[3] place without[4] her.

1. **as usual**
   照例；像往常一樣
2. **obey** [ə`beɪ] (v.)
   服從；遵守
3. **ugly** [`ʌglɪ] (a.)
   醜的；邪惡的
4. **without** [wɪð`aʊt] (prep.)
   沒有；無
5. **from then on** 從那時起
6. **stop at** 在……逗留
7. **pass right by**
   正好經過……
8. **no longer** 不再
9. **except** [ɪk`sept] (prep.)
   除……之外
10. **change** [tʃeɪndʒ] (v.)
    改變；使變化

From then on[5], Nello would never stop at[6] the mill. When walking to town, he would pass right by[7] it without even looking.

The boy no longer[8] had a friend in the world, except[9] Patrasche. And he was poor. There was nothing in the world that could change[10] that.

16

Old Jehan Daas often said to him, "We are poor. We must take what God sends[1]. The poor can't choose[2]."

The boy always listened in silence[3]. But in his heart remained[4] a small, sweet[5] hope[6]. A hope that he may one day be rich and famous.

1. **send** [send] (v.)
   發送；傳遞
   (send-sent-sent)
2. **choose** [tʃuːz] (v.)
   選擇；挑選
   (choose-chose-chosen)
3. **in silence** 沉默地
   （silence：寂靜）
4. **remain** [rɪ`meɪn] (v.)
   保持；繼續存在
5. **sweet** [swiːt] (a.) 甜美的

6. **hope** [houp] (n.)
   希望；盼望
7. **alone** [ə`loun] (a.)
   單獨的；獨自的
8. **say no** 拒絕
9. **artist** [`ɑːrtɪst] (n.)
   藝術家（尤指畫家）
10. **believe in** 相信；信任
11. **future** [`fjuːtʃər] (n.)
    未來；將來

"Sometimes the poor can choose," he said when he was alone[7] with Patrasche.
"They can choose to be great. Then people can no longer say no[8] to them."

He talked to Patrasche until late that evening about what a great artist[9] he would be.

Nello believed in[10] the future[11].

🎧 17

When the boy and the dog came home, old Jehan said, "Nello! Today is Alois' birthday, isn't it? Why aren't you at the party?"

"You're too[1] sick, grandfather. I can't leave you alone[2]."

1. **too** [tu:] (adv.) 太；過度
2. **leave . . . alone** 讓……單獨一個人
3. **nonsense** [ˋnɑːnsens] (n.) 胡說；胡鬧
4. **have an argument with** 和……爭執
5. **Not at all.** 一點也不
6. **to be honest** 坦白說
7. **invite** [ɪnˋvaɪt] (v.) 邀請
8. **surely** [ˋʃʊrli] (adv.) 確實；無疑
9. **wrong** [rɒːŋ] (a.) 錯誤的；不對的
10. **sigh** [saɪ] (v.) 嘆氣；嘆息
11. **yet** [jet] (conj.) 可是；然而

"Nonsense[3]! Have you had an argument with[4] Alois?"

"Not at all[5]. To be honest[6], Baas Cogez didn't invite[7] me this year. I don't think he likes me."

"But surely[8] you didn't do anything wrong[9]!"

"No! I drew a picture of Alois. That's all."

The old man sighed[10]. He had never been to school. Yet[11] he understood the world too well.

"Ah! You are very poor, my boy. So poor!"

"Yes, but I will be rich," he said, "in the future." And he believed it.

Today is Alois' birthday, **isn't it?**
今天是阿露薏絲的生日，對不對？

附加問句：在肯定的直述句後，用 n't 形成否定的附加問句，用來詢問事情或提出建議。

e.g. You respect your father, **don't you?**
你尊敬父親，對嗎？

A Match.

1 mill • • **a** a painting of a person

2 portrait • • **b** a building for grinding grain into flour

3 gift • • **c** almost certainly

4 secret • • **d** a present

5 probably • • **e** something that is only known by one person or a few people

B Replace with another word in the blank.

1 Alois was the poorest girl in the village.

⇨ _____

2 Alois' father was a soldier.

⇨ _____

3 When Baas Cogez saw Nello and Alois play together, he was very delighted.

⇨ _____

C Write down the name according to the description.

1 "He spends all of his time drawing." _____

2 "We are poor. We must take what God sends."

_____

3 "Sometimes the poor can choose." _____

D Choose the correct answer.

1 Nello hoped that one day he would be _____
   (a) rich and famous.

   (b) a great farmer.

   (c) a landowner.

2 Baas Cogez didn't want Nello to marry his daughter because _____
   (a) he was an artist.

   (b) he was dishonest.

   (c) he was poor and had never been to school.

3 Baas Cogez told his wife _____
   (a) to buy the picture of Alois.

   (b) to keep Nello away from Alois.

   (c) to give a silver coin to Nello.

Chapter Four

Hope

Nello had a secret that only Patrasche knew about.

There was an empty hut near his home. In this hut, Nello had drawn many sketches[1]. Nello couldn't buy any colors[2] but he found some charcoal[3] and chalk[4], and some rough[5] paper.

He could draw anything in black and white[6] and still make it look beautiful.

---

1. **sketch** [sketʃ] (n.)
   速寫；素描
2. **color** [`kʌlər] (n.) 顏料
3. **charcoal** [`tʃɑːrkoʊl] (n.)
   炭筆；炭條
4. **chalk** [tʃɔːk] (n.) 粉筆
5. **rough** [rʌf] (a.) 糙的
6. **in black and white**
   白紙黑字

Nello heard of a drawing contest[7]. Two hundred francs[8] would be given to the first-prize[9] winner[10]. Anybody under the age of eighteen could enter[11].

Nello believed that this was his opportunity[12] to improve[13] himself. So he began to work very hard, indeed[14].

Every evening, Patrasche would come into the hut and lie down[15]. He watched Nello work hard at drawing.

7. **contest** [`kɑːntest] (n.) 爭奪；競賽
8. **franc** [fræŋk] (n.) 法郎
9. **first-prize** 頭獎；冠軍
10. **winner** [`wɪnər] (n.) 獲勝者；優勝者
11. **enter** [`entər] (v.) 進入；參加
12. **opportunity** [ˌɑːpər`tuːnəti] (n.) 機會
13. **improve** [ɪm`pruːv] (v.) 改進；改善
14. **indeed** [ɪn`diːd] (adv.) 真正地；確實
15. **lie down** 躺下 (lie-lay-lain)

All spring, summer and autumn, Nello worked on[1] this drawing. He said nothing to anyone. His grandfather would not understand.

The drawings were due[2] on the first of December. The winner would be announced[3] on the twenty-fourth of that same month.

On the morning of the first, Nello loaded[4] his drawing onto[5] the cart. He left his work at the door of the city hall[6], as instructed[7].

60 *A Dog of Flanders*

"Maybe it's a terrible drawing," he thought. "I've never learned⁸ anything about art."

Nello walked home that day with many doubts⁹.

1. **work on** 致力於……
2. **due** [duː] (a.) 到期的
3. **announce** [əˋnaʊns] (v.) 宣佈；發佈
4. **load** [loʊd] (v.) 裝載；負載
5. **onto** [ˋɒntʊ] (prep.) 到……之上
6. **city hall** 市政廳
7. **as instructed** 遵照指示 (instruct：指示)
8. **learn** [lɜːrn] (v.) 學習；學會
9. **doubt** [daʊt] (n.) 懷疑；不相信

The winter was very bitter[1]. Pulling the milk cart was very hard work. Patrasche often slipped[2] on the icy[3] roads. Patrasche had become an old dog.

One day, Nello and Patrasche found a pretty puppet[4] in the snow. Nello tried to find its owner[5], but no one was around.

"This is a good present[6] for Alois," he thought.

1. **bitter** [ˋbɪtɚ] (a.)
   極冷的;嚴寒刺骨的
2. **slip** [slɪp] (v.) 滑跤;失足
3. **icy** [ˋaɪsi] (a.) 結冰的
4. **puppet** [ˋpʌpɪt] (n.) 玩偶
5. **owner** [ˋounɚ] (n.)
   主人;所有人
6. **present** [ˋprezənt] (n.) 禮物
7. **quietly** [ˋkwaɪətli] (adv.)
   輕聲地;安靜地
8. **climb up** 爬上
9. **knock** [nɑːk] (v.) 敲;擊
10. **thank** [θæŋk] (v.) 感謝

He quietly[7] climbed up[8] to her window and knocked[9] on it. Alois opened the window.

"Here is a doll I found in the snow," said Nello. "Take it."

With that, he went away quickly. Alois didn't even have a chance to thank[10] him.

Here is a doll **(which)** I found in the snow.
這個是我在雪地裡發現的玩偶。

當關係代名詞：在限定關係子句中，that 可以代替 which、who、whom。

e.g. Have you seen the book **(that)** I put on this table?
你有看到我放在這張桌上的書嗎？

That night, there was a big fire[1] at the mill. All the people in the village came out to put out[2] the fire.

The miller was furious[3]. "This fire was not an accident[4]!" he yelled[5]. "Somebody set this fire[6] on purpose[7]! And he'll pay for[8] it!"

Nello ran to the fire. He wanted to help. When he arrived[9] at the mill, Baas Cogez yelled at him.

1. **fire** [faɪr] (n.) 火
2. **put out** 熄滅
3. **furious** [`fjʊrɪəs] (a.) 狂怒的
4. **accident** [`æksədənt] (n.) 意外
5. **yell** [jɛl] (v.) 大喊；大叫
6. **set fire** 縱火
7. **on purpose** 故意；有目的地
8. **pay for** 因……受到懲罰；付出代價
9. **arrive** [ə`raɪv] (v.) 到達；抵達

"You! Nello! You know something about this fire, don't you? I saw you hanging around[10] here earlier today. I believe that you set this fire. I don't want to see you ever[11] again!"

From that day on, there was a rumor[12] in the village that Nello had started the fire. Many people thought that the boy was angry with Baas Cogez. And they believed that he had started the fire for revenge[13].

10. **hang around** 閒蕩;徘徊
    (hang-hung-hung)
11. **not . . . ever** 從來沒有……
    (= never)
12. **rumor** [`ru:mər] (n.)
    謠言;謠傳
13. **for revenge** 為了報復

The farmers didn't give Nello their milk anymore. The times were very difficult[1] for Nello and his family. They could no longer earn[2] money to buy food. They became very hungry. And the winter was very cold.

1. **difficult** [ˋdɪfɪkəlt] (a.)
   困難的；艱難的
2. **earn** [ɜːrn] (v.) 賺得
3. **if only** 只要……
4. **feel sorry about** . . .
   對……感到難過
5. **mean** [miːn] (a.)
   惡劣的；心地不好的

For Nello, the only thing that gave him hope was the drawing contest.

He thought, "If only[3] I could win, then they'd feel sorry about[4] being so mean[5] to me!"

Still[6], Nello tried[7] to understand his neighbors[8]. "Sometimes, people make mistakes[9]. I should forgive[10] them," he thought.

Old Jehan Daas became quite weak that winter.

6. **still** [stɪl] (adv.) 仍然；還是
7. **try** [traɪ] (v.) 試圖；努力
8. **neighbor** [ˋneɪbər] (n.) 鄰居
9. **make mistakes** 犯錯
10. **forgive** [fərˋgɪv] (v.)
　　原諒；寬恕
　　(forgive-forgave-forgiven)

A Fill in the blanks with the given words.

> puppet   opportunity   revenge

1 Nello believed that the drawing contest was his
_____ to improve himself.

2 One day, Nello and Patrasche found
a _____ in the snow.

3 People thought that Nello had started
the fire for _____.

B Rearrange the words to make a sentence.

1 All the people came out (to / fire / put / out / the).

_____

2 (only / the / thing / that) gave Nello hope was
the drawing contest.

_____

3 Nello thought, "People would feel sorry about
(so / to / mean / being / me)."

_____

C Choose the correct answer.

1 What is not true about the drawing contest?

(a) Only rich people could enter it.

(b) Two hundred francs would be given to the winner.

(c) The drawings were due on the first of December.

2 Why did Nello run to the fire?

(a) Because he wanted to rescue Alois.

(b) Because he wanted to help put out the fire.

(c) Because he wanted to comfort Baas Cogez.

3 Where did Nello draw many pictures?

(a) on the fields.

(b) in the churches.

(c) in an empty hut.

D Underline the wrong statements in the sentences.

1 The winner would be announced on Christmas day.

2 Pulling the cart was still easy for Patrasche.

3 It was true that Nello had started the fire.

4 After the fire, people were very nice to Nello.

Chapter Five

🎧 23 Christmas

Christmas was coming. The snow was six feet[1] deep[2]. Everyone loved that time of year. Even the poor people of the village had cakes and cookies to eat.

Nello and Patrasche were completely[3] alone. Old Jehan Daas had died a week before Christmas. He had died in his sleep. Patrasche and Nello were very sad. On the day of his funeral[4], they were the only ones who attended[5].

---

1. **feet** [fiːt] (n.) 呎
   （1 呎約等於 30 公分）
2. **deep** [diːp] (a.) 深的
3. **completely** [kəmˋpliːtli]
   (adv.) 完全地；徹底地

4. **funeral** [ˋfjuːnərəl] (n.)
   葬禮；喪葬
5. **attend** [əˋtend] (v.)
   參加；出席

Sadly, they would lose even their simple home. They didn't have enough money to pay[6] the rent[7]. The landlord[8] told them to get out[9]. Instead of[10] rent money, the landlord took everything that they had.

6. **pay** [peɪ] (v.) 付款；支付
7. **rent** [rent] (n.) 租金；租費
8. **landlord** [ˋlændlɔːrd] (n.) 房東；地主
9. **get out** 出去
10. **instead of . . .** 作為替代……

It was the night of the twenty-third of December. Nello and Patrasche slept[1] under the stars without[2] a blanket[3].

On the morning of Christmas Eve, they walked along the road to Antwerp. The winner of the prize was be announced at noon[4].

At noon, the doors of the building were opened. The crowd[5] ran into the hall[6].

As Nello entered the room, he saw a big drawing on the wall. It wasn't his own[7]. He hadn't won[8] the contest.

1. **sleep** [sli:p] (v.) 睡覺 (sleep-slept-slept)
2. **without** [wɪð`aʊt] (prep.) 沒有；無
3. **blanket** [`blæŋkɪt] (n.) 毛毯；毯子
4. **at noon** 在中午
5. **crowd** [kraʊd] (n.) 人群；群眾
6. **hall** [hɔl] (n.) 會堂；大廳
7. **own** [oʊn] (a.) 自己的
8. **win** [wɪn] (v.) 贏得；獲勝 (win-won-won)
9. **disappointed** [ˌdɪsə`pɔɪntɪd] (a.) 失望的；沮喪的
10. **all over** 結束

He was so disappointed[9], and said to Patrasche, "It's all over[10]."

The two started walking back to the village. They were hungry, sad and tired.

◦ The winner of the prize **was to be** announced at noon.
獲勝者將會在中午揭曉。

be + to + 原型動詞：用來說明已為未來某個時候安排好或計畫好的事件。

e.g. The president **is to make** a speech next week.
總統下星期要發表演講。

We **are to observe** the traffic rules. 我們要遵守交通規則。

Not a sound **was to be** heard. 一個聲音都沒有聽到。

Snow was falling fast[1]. It was terribly[2] cold on the way to[3] the village.

Suddenly, Patrasche smelled something strange. He stopped and started scratching at[4] the snow. He pulled out[5] a small brown leather[6] wallet[7].

On the front[8] of the case[9], the words BAAS COGEZ were written. Nello looked inside[10] the wallet. He found 2,000 francs.

He walked to the mill-house and knocked on the door.

1. **fast** [fæst] (adv.)
   迅速地;快速地
2. **terribly** [ˋterəbli] (adv.)
   很;非常
3. **on the way to**
   在……的途中
4. **scratch at**
   抓……;劃……
5. **pull out** 拔出
6. **leather** [ˋleðər] (a.)
   皮的;皮革製的
7. **wallet** [ˋwɑːlɪt] (n.)
   皮夾;錢包
8. **front** [frʌnt] (n.) 前面;正面
9. **case** [keɪs] (n.) 箱;套
10. **inside** [ɪnˋsaɪd] (prep.)
    在……裡面
11. **answer** [ˋænsər] (v.)
    回應;回答
12. **'d (=had) better**
    最好……
13. **leave** [liːv] (v.) 離開
14. **take out** 取出;拿出

When the miller's wife answered[11] the door, she was crying. "Poor boy. You'd better[12] leave[13] before my husband sees you. He's angry tonight. He lost a lot of money."

Nello took out[14] the wallet and gave it to her. "Patrasche found the money," he said.

"Please ask your husband to take care of my dog. He's old and weak. Please be good to this kind animal."

He kissed his dog and quickly left.

◦ On the front of the case, the words BAAS COGEZ were written.
在皮夾的前面寫著貝斯‧柯吉斯這幾個字。

被動式：be 動詞 + 過去分詞。想強調動作的承受者，或者動作的行為者未知或不重要，就可用被動語態。

e.g. The office is **locked** every evening.
辦公室每天晚上都上鎖。

Nello had saved[1] Alois and her family. If they had lost all that money, they would have been ruined[2].

The miller's wife led[3] the dog inside the house. Soon after[4], Baas Cogez entered through[5] the back door. He was very sad. "I can't find it. It's gone[6]."

Then, his wife laid[7] the wallet in his hands. She explained[8] to him how Patrasche and Nello found the wallet.

"I have been cruel[9] to that boy," he said at last[10].

"Nello and Patrasche should be with us on Christmas day. And every day after that, too. Let's go and find him in the morning."

The miller didn't know that Nello had no hut to sleep in that night.

---

1. **save** [seɪv] (v.) 救；挽救
2. **ruin** [ˋruɪn] (v.) 破產；破壞
3. **lead** [liːd] (v.) 引導；領路 (lead-led-led)
4. **soon after** 不久之後
5. **through** [θruː] (prep.) 穿越；通過
6. **be gone** 不見了 (lay-laid-laid)
7. **lay** [leɪ] (v.) 放；擱
8. **explain** [ɪkˋspleɪn] (v.) 解釋；說明
9. **cruel** [ˋkruːəl] (a.) 殘酷的；傷人的
10. **at last** 最後；終於

If they **had lost** all that money, they **would have been** ruined.

假如他們失去那筆錢，他們就破產了。

與過去事實相反的假設：If+ 子句主詞 + 過去完成式，主句主詞 +would/might/could/should + have + 過去分詞。

e.g. If the weather **had been** nice yesterday, we **would have gone** to the beach.

假如昨天天氣好的話，我們就會去海灘。

🎧 27

Baas Cogez and his family had dinner that evening. Patrasche wouldn't eat any food. He just lay down by[1] the door and cried.

Late in the evening, Patrasche ran out the door as a visitor[2] was entering the house.

1. **by** [baɪ] (prep.)
   在……旁邊；靠近
2. **visitor** [ˋvɪzɪtər] (n.) 訪客

The dog followed³ those footprints⁴ all the way to⁵ Antwerp. The streets of Antwerp were empty by this time⁶. Patrasche reached⁷ the steps⁸ of the big church. He climbed up the steps.

He saw one of the doors open. He walked in and found Nello inside the church. When the boy saw his dog, he put his arms around⁹ him.

3. **follow** [ˋfɑːloʊ] (v.) 跟隨
4. **footprint** [ˋfʊt͵prɪnt] (n.) 腳印；足跡
5. **all the way to** 一路到……
6. **by this time** 這次

7. **reach** [riːtʃ] (v.) 抵達；到達
8. **steps** [steps] (n.) 臺階
9. **put one's arms around** 擁抱……

28

"Let's lie down together and die," Nello cried out. "We aren't needed in this world."

The two lay down together on the floor. The boy and his dog thought about the good old days[1].

Then, the snow stopped falling. The moon came out from behind[2] the clouds. Moonlight[3] brightened the inside of the church for a moment[4].

Nello looked up[5] and clearly[6] saw the two paintings of the great Rubens. They were the paintings of Jesus suffering[7] on the cross[8].

1. **old days** 過去的日子
2. **behind** [bɪ`haɪnd] (prep.)
   在……後面;在……背後
3. **moonlight** [`muːnlaɪt] (n.)
   月光
4. **for a moment**
   一會兒;一下子

5. **look up** 抬頭往上看
6. **clearly** [`klɪrli] (adv.)
   清楚地
7. **suffer** [`sʌfər] (v.) 受苦
8. **cross** [krɒːs] (n.) 十字架

Nello stood up and stretched his arms out to them. Tears[9] streamed down on[10] his face.

"Oh, God!" he said.
"I've seen them at last[11].
It is enough! We will see His face soon."
The boy and the dog then fell asleep[12].

9. **tear** [tɪr] (n.) 眼淚
10. **stream down on** 流到……
11. **at last** 最後；終於
12. **fall asleep** 睡著
(fall-fell-fallen)

The next morning, people found the boy and the dog. They had frozen to death[1] in the middle of the night[2].

Throughout[3] the day, the townspeople[4] came to pay their respects[5] to Nello and Patrasche. Baas Cogez came with Alois, too.

"I was so cruel to that poor boy. I wish I could have made it up to[6] him."

1. **freeze to death** 凍死
   (freeze-froze-frozen)
2. **in the middle of the night**
   在半夜
3. **throughout** [θru:ˋaut]
   (prep.) 遍及；從頭到尾
4. **townspeople**
   [ˋtaunzˏpi:pəl]
   (n.) 市民；鎮民

5. **pay one's respect**
   表示尊敬；致意
6. **make it up to**
   對……作補償
7. **painter** [ˋpeɪntər] (n.) 畫家
8. **woodcutter** [ˋwudˏkʌtər]
   (n.) 伐木工人
9. **fallen** [fɔ:lən] (a.)
   倒下的；落下的

A famous painter[7] came to the church that day.

"I want to pay my respects to a great artist. That boy should have won the contest."

He carried Nello's drawing with him. It was a drawing of a simple woodcutter[8] sitting on a fallen[9] tree.

Nello was hugging Patrasche so tightly[10] that they could not be separated[11]. They rested[12] together peacefully in the ground.

10. **tightly** [ˋtaɪtli] (adv.) 緊緊地;牢固地
11. **separate** [ˋsepərət] (v.) 分隔;使分離
12. **rest** [rest] (v.) 安息;長眠

One Point Lesson

● **I wish I could have made it up to him.**
真希望我能夠補償他。

I wish:表示未能實現的願望。

e.g. **I wish you would stop making that noise.**
真希望你能停止發出那種噪音。
I wish I had eaten less. 真希望我吃得少一點。

A Fill in the blanks with the given words.

> alone   frozen   rent
> announced   explained

1. When old Jehan Daas died, Nello and Patrasche were completely _____.

2. Nello didn't have money to pay the _____.

3. The winner of the prize was to be _____ at noon.

4. Alois' mother _____ to Baas Cogez how Nello and Patrasche found his wallet.

5. Nello and Patrasche had _____ to death in the middle of the night.

B Match.

1. On the front of the wallet,   •   • ⓐ to take care of Patrasche.

2. Nello asked Alois' mother   •   • ⓑ the words Baas Cogez were written.

3. Nello clearly saw   •   • ⓒ all the way to Antwerp.

4. Patrasche followed the footprints   •   • ⓓ a present

C Choose the correct answer.

1 Why did Nello and Patrasche leave their house?

(a) Because Jehan Daas had died.

(b) Because Nello could not pay the rent.

(c) Because Nello stole the landlord's wallet.

2 Why did Nello go to Alois' house?

(a) To return the wallet.

(b) To see Alois.

(c) To say that he did not start the fire.

3 What did Baas Cogez regret after Nello had died?

(a) That he didn't invite Nello to the birthday party.

(b) That he didn't treat Nello more nicely.

(c) That he didn't buy more of Nello's art.

D True or False.

T F **1** The miller lost 2,000 francs and was ruined.

T F **2** Patrasche stayed at Alois' house for a few days.

T F **3** Patrasche ran out of the house and went to see Nello.

T F **4** Nello was hugging Patrasche very tightly when they were found.

Appendixes

1

Basic Grammar

要增強英文閱讀理解能力，應練習找出英文的主結構。
要擁有良好的英語閱讀能力，首先要理解英文的段落結構。

「英文的主要句型結構比較簡單」

所有的英語文章都是由主詞和動詞所構成的，無論文章再怎麼長或複雜，它的架構一定是「主詞和動詞」，而「補語」和「受詞」是做補充主詞和動詞的角色。

主詞　　動詞

某樣東西　　如何做
（人、事、物）

He runs (very fast).　　It is raining .

他　跑　（非常快）　　雨　正在下

主詞　　動詞　　補語　　（補充的話）

某樣東西　　如何做　　怎麼樣
（人、事、物）

This is a cat .　　The cat is very big .

這　是　一隻貓。　　那隻貓　是　非常　大

主詞	動詞	受詞

某樣東西 （人、事、物） ・ 如何做 ・ 什麼

> 人，事物， 兩者皆是受詞

I like you.

我 喜歡 你。

You gave me some flowers.

你 給 我 一些花

主詞	動詞	受詞	補語

某樣東西 （人、事、物） ・ 如何做 ・ 什麼 ・ 怎麼樣／什麼

You make me happy.

你 使（讓）我 幸福（快樂）

I saw him running.

我 看到 他 跑

其他修飾語或副詞等，都可以視為為了完成句子而臨時、額外、特別附加的，閱讀起來便可更加輕鬆；先具備這些基本概念，再閱讀《龍龍與忠狗》的部分精選篇章，最後做了解文章整體架構的練習。

Although Nello was a boy and Patrasche was a dog ,

雖然 龍龍 是 一位男孩 而 阿忠 是 一隻狗

they had a special friendship , closer to brotherhood.

他們 擁有 一份特別的友情 接近兄弟之情

They were both the same age .

他們 是 兩者 相同年紀

Yet, one seemed old and the other was young .

然而 一位 似乎是 老的 而 另一位 是 年輕的

They spent all of their time together.

他們 花費 他們全部的時間 在一起

Their home　　was　　a little hut　on the edge of a small village.
他們的家　　　是　　一間小屋　　　　　在一個小村莊旁

The village　　was　　near Antwerp.
這個村莊　　　是　　在安特衛普附近

It　　was surrounded　by cornfields and pastures.
它　　　加以圍繞　　　　被玉米田和牧場

In the center of the village　was　　a big windmill　.
在村莊的中央　　　　　　是　　一個大風車

A gray church　　stood　across from the windmill.
一座灰色的教堂　座落　　　在風車對面

At the top of the church, there　was　　an old clock　.
在教堂頂端　　　　　　　有　　一個老舊的鐘

The clock　　rang　every hour on the hour.
這座鐘　　　響　　每小時的整點

It　　made　a strange, empty sound　.
它　　發出　　一個淡漠空洞的聲音

To the villagers,　it　　seemed　like the saddest sound in the world.
對村民而言　　它　　似乎　　　像最悲傷的聲音　　在世界上

Nello and Patrasche　　lived　with a very old man.
龍龍與阿忠　　　　　住　　和一位上了年紀的男人

This man, Jehan Daas　,　was　Nello's grandfather.
這位男人叫耶漢・達斯　　是　　　龍龍的爺爺

He　　had　once　been　a soldier　.
他　　以前　　曾經是　一位軍人

Sadly, he was wounded in a war and was now crippled .
不幸地 他 受傷 在戰爭中 而且 是 現在 跛腿的

When Jehan Daas was eighty years old , his only daughter died .
當 耶漢・達斯 是 八十歲 他唯一的女兒 死了

The old man had no choice but to take care of his daughter's son.
這位老人 有 沒選擇 只好 照顧他女兒的兒子

The old man and the little boy , lived happily together.
這位老人和小男孩 住 快樂地在一起

They were very poor , but they had each other .
他們 是 很 貧窮 但 他們 擁有 彼此

That was enough .
那 是 足夠的

As for Patrasche, he kept the old man and little Nello happier .
至於阿忠 他 使 老人和小龍龍 更快樂

Patrasche, a dog of Flanders , was a slave once.
阿忠，法蘭德斯的一隻狗 是 一個奴隸 以前

His owner forced him to pull a cart full of iron.
他的主人 強迫 他 拉貨車 裝滿鐵礦

One summer day, Patrasche was very thirsty when he
一個夏日 阿忠 是 很 渴 當 他

was working .
正在工作時

But he wasn't allowed to stop and drink .
但是 他 不被允許 停下來喝水

After some walking, he became dizzy and fell down .
走了一會兒後 他 變成 頭暈的 然後 倒下來

2 Guide to Listening Comprehension

 When listening to the story, use some of the techniques shown below. If you take time to study some phonetic characteristics of English, listening will be easier.

Get in the flow of English.

English creates a rhythm formed by combinations of strong and weak stress intonations. Each word has its particular stress that combines with other words to form the overall pattern of stress or rhythm in a particular sentence.

When you are speaking and listening to English, it is essential to get in the flow of the rhythm of English. It takes a lot of practice to get used to such a rhythm. So, you need to start by identifying the stressed syllable in a word.

Listen for the strongly stressed words and phrases.

In English, key words and phrases that are essential to the meaning of a sentence are stressed louder. Therefore, pay attention to the words stressed with a higher pitch. When listening to an English recording for the first time, what matters most is to listen for a general understanding of what you hear. Do not try to hear every single word. Most of the unstressed words are articles or auxiliary verbs, which don't play an important role in the general context. At this level, you can ignore them.

Pay attention to liaisons.

In reading English, words are written with a space between them. There isn't such an obvious guide when it comes to listening to English. In oral English, there are many cases when the sounds of words are linked with adjacent words.

For instance, let's think about the phrase "**take off**," which can be used in "take off your clothes." "Take off your clothes" doesn't sound like [teɪk ɔːf] with each of the words completely and clearly separated from the others. Instead, it sounds as if almost all the words in context are slurred together, [ˈteɪkɔːf], for a more natural sound.

Shadow the voice of the native speaker.

Finally, you need to mimic the voice of the native speaker. Once you are sure you know how to pronounce all the words in a sentence, try to repeat them like an echo. Listen to the book again, but this time you should try a fun exercise while listening to the English.

This exercise is called "shadowing." The word "shadow" means a dark shade that is formed on a surface. When used as a verb, the word refers to the action of following someone or something like a shadow. In this exercise, pretend you are a parrot and try to shadow the voice of the native speaker.

Try to mimic the reader's voice by speaking at the same speed, with the same strong and weak stresses on words, and pausing or stopping at the same points.

Experts have already proven this technique to be effective. If you practice this shadowing exercise, your English speaking and listening skills will improve by leaps and bounds. While shadowing the native speaker, don't forget to pay attention to the meaning of each phrase and sentence.

Listen to what you want to shadow many times. Start out by just trying to shadow a few words or a sentence.

 Mimic the CD out loud. You can shadow everything the speaker says as if you are singing a round, or you also can speak simultaneously with the recorded voice of the native speaker.

 As you practice more, try to shadow more. For instance, shadow a whole sentence or paragraph instead of just a few words.

3 Listening Guide

以下為《龍龍與忠狗》各章節的前半部。一開始若能聽清楚發音，之後就沒有聽力的負擔。先聽過摘錄的章節，之後再反覆聆聽括弧內單字的發音，並仔細閱讀各種發音的説明。以下都是以英語的典型發音為基礎，所做的簡易説明，即使這裡未提到的發音，也可以配合音檔反覆聆聽，如此一來聽力必能更上層樓。

Chapter One page 16 🎧 30

Although Nello (❶) ( ) boy and Patrasche was a dog, they had a special (❷), closer to brotherhood. They were both the same age. Yet, one seemed old and the other was young. They (❸) all of their time together. Their home was a (❹) hut on the edge of a small village.

❶ **was a:** was 與 a 產生連音，發出 wasa 的音，聽起來像是單獨一個字的發音。

❷ **friendship:** friendship 兩個音節的母音中間為 -ndsh- 的子音組合，-d 音會迅速略過，中間會有一短暫停頓。

❸ **spent:** s 音後面接無聲子音 [p]、[t]、[k] 時，無聲子音會轉變為有聲子音。所以 spent 中的 [p] 音會轉變為 [b] 音。

❹ **little:** little 中的 -tt 發音為 [t] 音，但加上「l」音會形成帶有 [r] 音的發音。

Old Jehan Daas became very weak. It was (❶) for him to go out (❷) (   ) cart anymore. So little Nello collected money at the markets.
He (❸) hard and honestly. The farmers were happy to do business with (❹) (   ) fine, hardworking boy.

❶ **impossible:** impossible 的發音為 [ɪmˋpɑːsəbəl]，重音在第二音節，所以相對重音節的周圍音節會聽不清楚其發音。如 im- 的發音常會聽不到或聽不清楚其發音。

❷ **with the:** with 中的 -th 的發音會和 the 重複 [ð] 音，所以 [ð] 音只發一次。這個發音規則如同 summer 這個字，m 重複兩次，但只發一次音。

❸ **worked:** 於 [p]、[k]、[s]、[sh] 等無聲子音後面加上 -ed，則 -ed 發 [t] 音。另外，work 和 walk 聽起來發音相似，但只要仔細聆聽便可以分辨此兩個音有無捲舌的不同。

❹ **such a:** such 和 a 連在一起唸時，會形成連音 [sʌtʃə]，所以整個字聽起來像是單獨一個字的發音。

Eventually, Nello told his secret to (❶) person. That person was a little girl who lived nearby. Her name was Alois. She (❷) (   ) a red mill. Her father, Baas Cogez, was the miller. He was (❸) (   ) rich man. Little Alois was a pretty girl.

❶ **another:** another 整個字的發音為 [əˋnʌðər]，重音在第二音節，相對的鄰近音節的音會微弱而聽不清楚，加上第一音節的 a 又是母音，更加聽不到其發音。這是英語發音的顯著特點之一。

❷ **lived in:** lived 的發音為 [lɪvd]，會和後面的 in 成為連音，所以這兩個字一起唸的發音為 [lɪvdɪn]。

❸ **quite a:** quite 的發音為 [kwaɪt]，[t] 音會和後面的 a 形成連音 [tə]，聽起來像是只有一個字的發音。

Chapter Four page 58 🎧33

Nello had a secret that only Patrasche knew about. There was an empty hut near his home. In this hut, Nello (❶) (   ) many sketches. Nello (❷) (   ) any colors but he found some charcoal and chalk, and some rough paper. He could draw anything in black and white and still (❸) (   ) look beautiful.

❶ had drawn: had 的 [d] 音和 drawn 的 [d] 音重複,所以只發一次。had 的 [d] 音省略不發,而中間會有一個小停頓。

❷ couldn't buy: couldn't 和後面的 buy 一起發音時,[t] 音會迅速略過,不發出來,中間會有一短暫的小停頓。

❸ make it: make 的 [k] 會與後面的 it 形成連音,所以這兩個字會發的音。同理可證,made it 會發 [meɪdɪt] 的音。

Chapter Five page 70 🎧 34

Christmas was coming. The snow was six feet deep. Everyone loved that time of year. Even the poor people of the village had (❶) ( ) ( ) to eat. Nello and Patrasche were (❷) alone. Old Jehan Daas had died a week before Christmas. He had died in his sleep. Patrasche and Nello were very sad. On the day of his funeral, they were the only ones who attended.

❶ cakes and cookies: cake 的 [k] 音迅速略過而聽不出其發音,cakes 的 [s] 音會與 and 形成連音 [sænd]。and 的 [d] 音也會迅速略過而聽不出其發音。

❷ completely: 重音在第二音節,-letely 中的 [t] 音會迅速略過,中間會有一極短暫的停頓。

4

Listening Comprehension

🎧 35 (A) Listen to the CD and fill in the blanks.

1 His owner kicked Patrasche into a _____.

2 Patrasche decided that Jehan Daas would never again _____ the cart.

3 Jehan Daas put the _____ around Patrasche's shoulders.

4 The drawing contest was the only _____ for Nello.

5 The winner was _____ on the twenty-fourth of December.

6 Nello and Patrasche had _____ to death in the middle of the night.

(B) True or False.

🎧 36 T F 1

....

T F 2

....

T F 3

....

T F 4

....

37

C Write down the question and choose the correct answer.

1 _____?

    (a) That Nello wanted to become a great artist.

    (b) That Nello loved Alois.

    (c) That Nello had started the fire at the mill.

2 _____?

    (a) That he hadn't invited Nello to the birthday party.

    (b) That he hadn't treated him more nicely.

    (c) That he hadn't bought a drawing from Nello.

D Match.

1 _____ • • **a** to take care of Patrasche.

2 _____ • • **b** that only Patrasche knew about.

3 _____ • • **c** in order to see the Rubens paintings.

4 _____ • • **d** that they could not be separated.

Translation

薇達（Ouida,1839–1908）為英國女性小說家，出生於英國，父親為英國人，母親為法國人。她真正的名字是 Marie Louise de la Ramee，筆名由牙牙學語時的乳名「露薏絲」而來。她二十多歲時開始寫作，三十歲移居義大利後不曾回到倫敦。

薇達喜愛動物，寫了許多關於動物的小說，也在家中養了幾隻狗。創作孩童相關的小說使她逐漸成名與致富。

她事業有成，卻因不善理財，在窮困中逝世。薇達終生未婚，創作大量佳作，如《紐倫堡的爐子》（*The Nurnberg Stove*）和《龍龍與忠狗》（*A Dog of Flanders*）。

故事介紹

【譯注：本書主角人物譯名，採用 1979 年於華視播出的日本卡通《龍龍與忠狗》之譯名。】

主角龍龍（Nello）與祖父和領養的狗阿忠（Patrasche）同住，雖然貧窮卻甘之如飴。龍龍具有天分，希望成為藝術家。他盡全力完成畫作，參加村裡的繪畫比賽。但好景不長，爺爺過世加上比賽落選，他的生命走向絕望。

由於極度渴望一睹魯本斯的畫作，他和阿忠在聖誕夜前往教堂，終於看見了他最喜歡的一幅畫作。然而，隔日清晨，在畫作前，人們發現了死去的男孩與狗。

這是關於窮人和對動物同情心的故事。直到今日，由於書中比利時的自然景致、精細的角色描寫與架構良好的劇情，仍廣愛讀者喜愛。

故事場景設定在安特衛普，是比利時的第二大城市。安特衛普有許多有趣的景點適合觀光與欣賞自然風光，例如馬克斯廣場的老舊火車站，和名為霍博肯的美麗小村。

然而，最有名的還是故事主場景的聖母主教座堂，教堂內收藏許多魯本斯的原創畫作，包含龍龍渴求一窺的《上十字架》（*Elevation of the Cross*）及《下十字架》（*Descent from the Cross*）。

[第一章] 龍龍與阿忠

p. 16–17 雖然龍龍是一個小男孩，而阿忠是一條狗，但他們之間存在著特別的友情，接近兄弟之情。

他們年紀相同，然而，一個似乎老了，而另一個還很年輕。他們無時無刻都形影不離，住在小村莊旁的一個小屋。

這個村莊在安特衛普附近，四周環繞玉米田和牧場。

村莊的中央是一個大風車，一棟灰色的教堂座落於風車對面。

教堂頂有座古老的鐘，這座鐘每小時的整點會敲響，聲音淡漠空洞，對村民來說似乎像是世上最悲傷的聲音。

p. 18–19 龍龍與阿忠和一位老人住在一起，這老人叫做耶漢·達斯，是龍龍的祖父。

他以前是軍人，在戰爭中不幸受了傷現在跛腳。耶漢·達斯八十歲時，他唯一的女兒過世了。

這位老人別無選擇，只得照顧他女兒的兒子。老人和小男孩快樂地住在一起。雖然他們很窮，但他們擁有彼此，這樣便足夠了。

至於阿忠，他讓老人和小男孩都更加快樂。

p. 20–21 阿忠是在法蘭德斯的一隻狗，牠曾是奴隸，主人強迫牠拉載裝滿鐵礦的貨車。

有個夏日，阿忠工作得非常口渴，但是主人不准牠停下來喝水。

走了一會兒之後，牠頭暈倒下了。牠的主人跑過去鞭打牠，阿忠無法動彈，主人把牠踢進了水溝裡才罷手。

一會兒過後，一位老人和小男孩看到阿忠。

「我們不能讓如此漂亮的狗兒死去，」老人說道。他將這隻狗拖回他的小屋。

這就是老耶漢・達斯、小龍龍和阿忠相遇的情景。

p. 22–23 老人和小龍龍無微不至地照顧阿忠，而且還寵愛著牠。他們輕柔地摸牠的頭，並鋪了一張床給牠睡覺。

第一次，阿忠感覺到愛，這種感覺對牠來說很陌生但很美妙。牠決定要趕快康復好報答他們的仁慈，牠想要照顧他們。

當牠終於站起來時，牠吠了幾聲，伸長了雙腿，龍龍和老人歡欣地手舞足蹈，擁抱狗兒。

p. 24–25 阿忠走到小貨車那裡，牠知道小貨車是老人的謀生工具。

老耶漢・達斯運載農人的牛奶罐到安特衛普的市場，他幫農夫們賣牛奶，再把空罐子拿回來。農夫們會給他一些利潤賺。

阿忠決定再也不讓老人拉這麼重的貨車，阿忠站在小貨車旁好幾天。最後，他開始用牙齒來拉車。

「好啦，好！」老耶漢・達斯喊道。

「我知道我說服不了你不要拉車。」

老人把挽具放在阿忠的肩上，阿忠很高興做這個工作。和他過去的工作相比，這是份輕鬆的工作。

[第二章] 幾年之後

p. 28-29 老耶漢·達斯身體變得虛弱，他已經沒辦法再和小貨車一同出門，所以由小龍龍到市場收錢。

小龍龍工作努力且實在，農夫都很高興和這麼善良又努力的男孩做生意。

下午時分，他們兩個回到家裡。阿忠會卸下挽具，高興地吠叫。

龍龍會和祖父閒聊當天的生意。他們會一起吃著簡單的餐點，老耶漢·達斯會說著他當年當軍人時的有趣故事，他們都笑得很開心。

p. 30-31 許多年過去了，他們還是過得很開心。法蘭德斯並非是一個美麗的地方，除了玉米田和農場之外，就沒有其他可觀賞的了。

然而，其簡單之美就足以讓男孩和他的狗兒倘佯其中了。他們無法想像世界上還有比這裡更美的地方。

冬季時節，生活的確更艱難，但他們從不抱怨天氣嚴寒。

他們簡單的小屋已夠溫暖，他們不在意貧窮，他們擁有彼此，這也就足夠了。

p. 32-33 只有一件事是阿忠不喜歡的。

安特衛普是個充滿老教堂的城市，各地都有一座教堂，教堂裡可以看到魯本斯的傑作。

魯本斯是優秀的畫家，也是偉大的大師，他是當地人唯一敬仰的人。

現在阿忠的煩惱是：龍龍也崇拜魯本斯。小男孩常常消失走進教堂裡，這可憐的狗兒就得在外頭的嚴寒中等待。

等小男孩回來時，他總是顯得滿臉悲傷。

「但願我能看到它們就好了，阿忠！」他會如此說道。「它們」是什麼？阿忠無從得知。

p. 34–35 他們是教堂裡兩幅被布遮蓋的圖畫。

小男孩正在哭泣。

「真悲慘，我無法看到那些畫，只因為我窮，付不起！魯本斯畫了那些圖是要給每個人欣賞，而不是只為了富人。」

他無法看到那些畫，而阿忠也無法幫助他。假如要欣賞它們，必須支付一個銀幣。那比龍龍一個月存的錢還多。

小龍龍強烈地喜愛藝術。當這個小男孩走過城鎮時，他驚豔於他所見到的美麗。他會注目著一座簡單的教堂或風車，欣賞它的美麗。

p. 36 雖然龍龍從來不曾上過學，但他很聰明。沒有人教他如何唸書，也沒有人教他如何畫畫。事實上，沒有人教他任何事，他擁有人們所謂的「天賦」。

沒有人知道這件事，甚至連他自己也不知道，只有阿忠明白。那隻聰明的大狗注意到男孩在石頭上畫畫，當他看著美麗的夕陽時，他常看著龍龍的臉龐閃耀著光芒。

p. 38–39 男孩心理默默想成為一位偉大的畫家，然而，他從沒有告訴任何人，而耶漢·達斯希望他做其他事。

他想要小孫子當農夫，他認為男人都該成為純樸的農夫。對

老人而言，成為農夫是世上最成功的事情。

　　然而，龍龍一點也不想成為農夫，但他無法告訴老人，那會傷他的心。

　　有時在晚上，龍龍會在阿忠的耳旁低語他的夢想，阿忠是唯一能了解他的人，其他人都無從得知。所以他和阿忠保守著這個秘密。

[第三章] 一位小女孩

p. 44–45　終於，龍龍把他的秘密告訴另一個人，那是個住在附近的小女孩，名叫阿露薏絲，她住在一個紅磨坊裡。

　　她的父親貝斯‧柯吉斯是磨坊主人，他相當有錢。小阿露薏絲是個美麗的女孩，有著深色的眼睛和明亮紅潤的雙頰。

　　小阿露薏絲常和龍龍與阿忠玩耍，他們在原野上摘雛菊和莓果，他們一起去古老的灰色教堂裡，也一起在雪中奔跑。

　　阿露薏絲是村中最富裕的小女孩，城中的人都夢想著兒子能娶到她。

p. 46–47　當龍龍、阿露薏絲和阿忠在原野時，龍龍畫了一幅阿露薏絲的肖像。

　　那時，貝斯‧柯吉斯正好走過原野，他看到龍龍和阿露薏絲在那裡時，他非常生氣。

　　「阿露薏絲，」他大喊。「你為什麼在這裡玩耍？趕快回家！」

接著，貝斯‧柯吉斯拿起阿露薏絲的畫像，龍龍的臉漲紅了起來。

「我畫我看到的所有事物，」他説。

「這裡，我給你這銀幣買這張畫，花時間畫畫很愚蠢，但我很喜歡這張畫。」

「請把這張畫當作禮物，」龍龍説。

龍龍穿越原野離開了。

「有了那些錢，我就可以去看魯本斯的畫作，」他和阿忠説道：「但我就是不能賣她的畫。」

p. 48-49 貝斯‧柯吉斯那晚回到磨坊。

「龍龍不能這麼常和阿露薏絲玩，」他對妻子説。

「他現在十五歲，而她十二歲。再過幾年，他可能就會娶她。他只是一位從沒上過學的窮小子。」

「可是他是一位善良誠實的男孩，」妻子説道。

「的確，」磨坊主人説道：「但他花去所有的時間畫畫，他絕不可能像我一樣成為地主。聽著，你必須讓那個男孩遠離阿露薏絲，要不然我就會把她送到遙遠的女修道院去。」

隔天，她告訴阿露薏絲不要再和龍龍玩耍了。然而，阿露薏絲並沒有聽她的話。

p. 50-51 幾天之後，阿露薏絲照常去找龍龍。當她把手放到他的手上時，龍龍説：「不，阿露薏絲，我們不應該讓你爸爸生氣。他不要你和窮小子玩耍。他是個好人，我們該聽他的話。」

龍龍很難過地説出這些話，這世界要是沒有她，將會醜陋得多。

從那時起，龍龍從不在磨坊那裡停留。走到城鎮時，他就只是路過，甚至沒有瞧它一眼。

在這世界上，除了阿忠外，這男孩就沒有其他朋友，他是個窮人，這世界上沒有東西可以改變這事實。

p. 52–53 老耶漢‧達斯常告訴他，「我們是窮人。我們必須接受上帝的安排，窮人無從選擇。」

男孩總是靜靜地聽，但他的心仍有一個小小的甜美希望，希望有天他能變得富裕且出名。

「有時窮人可以選擇，」當他與阿忠獨處時說道：「他們能選擇成為偉大的人，這樣人們就不會再拒絕他們。」

那晚，他和阿忠說話說到很晚，訴說他要成為一位怎麼樣的偉大畫家。

龍龍相信有美好的未來。

p. 54–55 男孩和狗兒回到家時，老耶漢說道，「龍龍！今天是阿露薏絲的生日，對吧？你為什麼沒有去舞會呢？」

「你病得太重了，爺爺，我不能留下你一個人。」

「胡說！你和阿露薏絲吵架了嗎？」

「才沒有呢，老實說，貝斯‧柯吉斯今年沒有邀請我，我想他不喜歡我吧。」

「但你實在沒有做錯任何事！」

「不！我畫了一張阿露薏絲的畫像，就這樣。」

老人嘆了口氣。他從沒有上過學，然而他很了解這世界。

「噢！你真可憐，我的男孩。真可憐！」

「沒錯，但我會變有錢的，」他說道，「在以後。」他如此深信著。

111

[第四章] 希望

p. 58–59 龍龍有個秘密,這個秘密只有阿忠知道。

在他家附近有一個空的小屋。在小屋中,龍龍畫了許多素描。龍龍買不起任何顏料,但他找到一些炭筆、粉筆和一些粗糙的紙。

他可以用黑白畫任何東西,而且還能畫得很好看。

龍龍聽到了繪畫比賽的消息,冠軍得主會得到兩百法郎,年齡十八歲以下的人能參加。

龍龍相信這是他提高自己身價的機會。所以他確實開始勤奮努力。

每天晚上,阿忠會來到小屋躺下,看著龍龍努力地畫畫。

p. 60–61 整個春天、夏天和秋天,龍龍都致力於這張畫,他沒有和任何人說話,他的爺爺不會了解其原因。

繪畫比賽的期限為十二月一日,獲勝者將會在當月的二十四日公佈。

在十二月一日早上,龍龍用貨車裝載他的畫,按照指示放到市政廳的門口。

「也許它是一幅很糟的畫,」他想道:「我從來沒有學過美術。」

那天,龍龍帶著許多懷疑返家。

p. 62–63 冬天非常酷寒,拉牛奶車是非常辛苦的工作。阿忠常在結冰的路上滑跤,牠已經是一條老狗了。

有一天,龍龍和阿忠在雪中看到一個漂亮的洋娃娃,龍龍試圖尋找它的主人,但沒有人在附近。

「這可以給阿露薏絲當禮物，」他想道。

他偷偷地爬上她的窗戶，敲她的窗，阿露薏絲打開窗戶。「這是我在雪地裡發現的洋娃娃，」龍龍說道：「給你。」

話說畢，他便迅速離開。阿露薏絲甚至來不及向他道謝。

p. 64–65 那天晚上，磨坊發生了一場大火，村裡全部都的人跑出來滅火。

磨坊主人很生氣。「這場火不是意外！」他大喊。「是有人故意縱火！他會受到懲罰的！」

龍龍跑到火場想要幫忙。他到達磨坊時，貝斯‧柯吉斯對他大喊。

「就是你！龍龍！你知道這場火的內幕，對吧？我看到你今天稍早在這附近閒晃。我想縱火的人一定是你，我不想再看到你了！」

從那天起，龍龍縱火的謠言便在村裡傳開。許多人認為他對貝斯‧柯吉斯心存不滿，所以認為他欲報復而縱了火。

p. 66–67 農夫們不再給龍龍牛奶了，日子對龍龍和家人而言非常艱難，他們不能再賺錢買食物。他們很餓，冬天又很寒冷。

對龍龍而言，唯一能給予他希望的就是繪畫比賽。

他想道，「只要我獲勝了，他們就會因為對我如此惡劣而感到抱歉！」

龍龍仍然試著體諒鄰居。「人們有時總會犯錯，我應該原諒他們，」他想道。

那個冬天，老耶漢‧達斯愈來愈虛弱了。

113

[第五章] 聖誕節

p. 70-71 聖誕節即將來臨，積雪已有六吋深。人人都喜歡一年當中的這個時節，即使是村中的窮人都有蛋糕和餅乾可吃。

龍龍和阿忠極度孤單，老耶漢‧達斯於聖誕節的前一星期於睡夢中去世了。阿忠和龍龍很難過，在他出殯的那天，他們是唯一出席的人。

令人傷心的是，他們甚至就要失去簡陋的家了。他們不夠錢付房租，地主趕他們出去，每樣東西都被拿去抵壓房租。

p. 72-73 這天是十二月二十三日的晚上，龍龍和阿忠在星空下睡覺，沒有蓋任何棉被。

在聖誕節前夕的早晨，他們沿路走到安特衛普，獲勝者將會在中午宣佈。

中午時分，市政廳的門大開了，群眾跑進大廳裡。龍龍進去看到牆上掛著一幅大型繪畫，那不是他的畫，他沒有贏得比賽。

他很失望，對阿忠說道，「結束了。」

他們兩個踏上返回村莊的歸途，滿是飢餓、難過和疲累。

p. 74-75 雪下得很大，返回村莊之路極為嚴寒。突然，阿忠聞到個奇怪的味道，牠停下來，開始用爪子抓雪地，拔出了一個小的褐色皮夾。

在皮夾的前面有「貝斯‧柯吉斯」這幾個字刻在上面。龍龍發現皮夾裡有兩千元法郎。

他走到磨坊屋敲門，磨坊主人的妻子來應門，她大叫：「可憐的孩子，你最好趁我丈夫看到你之前走開。他今晚很生氣，他掉了很多錢。」

龍龍拿出皮夾交給她。「阿忠發現這些錢，」他說道。

「請交代您的丈夫照顧我的狗，牠又老又虛弱。請一定要善待這隻善良的動物。」

他親了他的狗兒後便迅速離開。

p. 76–77　龍龍救了阿露薏絲和她的家人，假如他們失去這些錢就會破產。

磨坊主人的太太帶這隻狗到屋內。不久，貝斯·柯吉斯從後門進來。他很難過，「我找不到，它不見了。」

然後，他的妻子把皮夾放在他手裡，向他說明阿忠和龍龍如何發現皮夾。

「我對那男孩太殘忍了，」他最後說道。

「龍龍和阿忠應該和我們一起過聖誕節，還有以後的每一天也是，我們早上就去找他。」磨坊主人不知道龍龍那晚已經無處可棲身了。

p. 78–79　那天晚上，貝斯·柯吉斯和他的家人一起用餐，阿忠沒有吃任何東西，牠只是躺在門邊發出叫聲。

較晚的時候，當訪客進入屋內時，阿忠跑出屋外。

狗兒跟隨著腳印一路來到安特衛普，此時安特衛普的街道空蕩無人。阿忠到達大教堂階梯，爬上階梯。

牠看到有一扇門是開著的，走進去發現龍龍在教堂裡。男孩看見他的狗兒時便與牠相擁在一起。

p. 80–81 「我們一起躺著死去吧，」龍龍大喊：「我們不被世界所需要。」

他們兩個一起躺在地板上，男孩和狗兒想到過去美好的日子。

然後，雪停了，月亮從雲層後露臉，月光片刻之間照亮教堂內部。

龍龍往上看，清楚地看到了偉大的魯本斯的兩幅畫作，畫中描繪了耶穌在十字架上受苦的景象。

龍龍站起來伸出雙臂，眼淚滑落臉龐。

「噢，天啊！」他說道。

「我終於看到它們了。這樣就足夠了！我們不久就會看到『他』的面容。」

然後，男孩和狗兒便睡著了。

p. 82–83 隔天早上，人們發現男孩和狗兒，他們在半夜凍死了。這天，鎮民都來向龍龍和阿忠致敬。貝斯．柯吉斯也和阿露薏絲來到這裡。

「我對那位小男孩這麼殘忍，我真希望可以做些事補償他。」

那天，一位知名的畫家來到教堂。「我要向一位偉大畫家致上敬意，這位男孩應該贏得比賽。」他拿著龍龍的畫作，上面描繪一位樸實的伐木工人坐在一棵倒下的樹上。

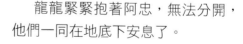

龍龍緊緊抱著阿忠，無法分開，他們一同在地底下安息了。

Answers

P. 26   **A**   cart, dizzy

       B   **1** love   **2** pull   **3** empty

P. 27   **C**   **1** F   **2** F   **3** T   **4** F   **5** T

       D   **1** surrounded   **2** windmill   **3** church
            4 clock

P. 40   **A**   **1** honest   **2** disappear   **3** imagine
            4 enough

       B   **1** T   **2** F   **3** F

P. 41   **C**   **1** Jehan Daas   **2** Nello   **3** Rubens

       D   **1** (c)   **2** (a)

P. 56   **A**   **1** - (b)   **2** - (a)   **3** - (d)   **4** - (e)   **5** - (c)

       B   **1** richest   **2** miller   **3** angry

P. 57   **C**   **1** Baas Cogez   **2** Jehan Daas   **3** Nello

       D   **1** (a)   **2** (c)   **3** (b)

P. 68   **A**   **1** opportunity   **2** puppet   **3** revenge

       B   **1** to put out the fire   **2** The only thing that
            3 being so mean to me

P. 69　C　**1** (a)　　**2** (b)　　**3** (c)

D　**1** Christmas day　**2** still easy　**3** true
4 very nice

P. 84　A　**1** alone　　**2** rent　　**3** announced
4 explained　**5** frozen

B　**1** - ⓑ　　**2** - ⓐ　　**3** - ⓓ　　**4** - ⓒ

P. 85　C　**1** (b)　　**2** (a)　　**3** (b)

D　**1** F　**2** F　**3** T　**4** T

P. 100　A　**1** ditch　**2** pull　**3** harness　**4** hope
5 announced　　**6** frozen

B　**1** Jehan Daas wanted Nello to become a soldier.
(F)
2 Baas Cogez thought that Nello had stolen his
wallet. (F)
3 Nello could draw anything in black and white
and make it beautiful. (T)
4 Nello was sure that he could win the contest. (F)

P. 101　C　**1** What secret did Nello and Patrasche have?　(a)
2 What did Baaz Cogez regret after Nello had
died? (b)

D　**1** Nello was hugging Patrasche so tightly　- ⓓ
2 Nello asked the miller's wife　- ⓐ
3 People had to pay a silver coin　- ⓒ
4 Nello had a secret　- ⓑ

Adaptors of "*A Dog of Flanders*!"

David Desmond O'Flaherty

University of Carleton (Honors English Literature and Language)
Kwah-Chun Foreign Language High School,
English Conversation Teacher

龍龍與忠狗【二版】
A Dog of Flanders

作者 _ 薇達（Ouida）

改寫 _ David Desmond O'Flaherty

插圖 _ Petra Hanzak

翻譯 / 編輯 _ 劉心怡

作者 / 故事簡介翻譯 _ 王采翎

校對 _ 楊維芯

封面設計 _ 林書玉

排版 _ 葳豐／林書玉

播音員 _ Nancy Kim, Sean Logan

製程管理 _ 洪巧玲

發行人 _ 周均亮

出版者 _ 寂天文化事業股份有限公司

電話 _ +886-2-2365-9739

傳真 _ +886-2-2365-9835

網址 _ www.icosmos.com.tw

讀者服務 _ onlineservice@icosmos.com.tw

出版日期 _ 2019年10月 二版一刷（250201）

郵撥帳號 _ 1998620-0 寂天文化事業股份有限公司

國家圖書館出版品預行編目資料

龍龍與忠狗【二版】/ Ouida 著；David Desmond
O'Flaherty 改寫. 一二版. 一[臺北市]：寂天文化,
2019.10 面；公分. (Grade 2經典文學讀本)譯自：
A Dog of Flanders

ISBN　978-986-318-847-6 (25K平裝附光碟片)

1. 英語　2. 讀本

805.18　　　　　　　　　　　　108016084